First edition for the United States and its dependencies, Canada, and the Philippines
published by Barron's Educational Series, Inc., 2002.

All inquiries should be addressed to:
Barron's Educational Series, Inc.
250 Wireless Boulevard
Hauppauge, New York 11788
http://www.barronseduc.com

Devised and produced by Tucker Slingsby Ltd
Berkeley House
73 Upper Richmond Road
London SW15 2SZ
England

International Standard Book No. 0-7641-5486-9

Library of Congress Catalog Card No. 2001093897

Printed in Singapore by KHL Printing, Singapore
9 8 7 6 5 4 3 2 1

Color reproduction by Bright Arts Graphics, Singapore

I Want to Play!

Sue Robinson

illustrated by
Andy Beckett

BARRON'S

One morning Bonnie woke up very early. Her mother and her sisters and her brother were still fast asleep.

Bonnie wriggled and wiggled but no one woke up.
"I want to play!" she said, but no one stirred.

So Bonnie crept out of the basket and slipped through the kitchen door.

Bonnie had never been outside before. The garden looked very exciting! She saw the birds on the lawn.

"Play with me!"called Bonnie as she ran toward the birds. But they flew away and wouldn't come down to play.

"Never mind," said Bonnie.
"There are lots of other things to see."

A web of sparkly thread caught
her eye. Something pretty
to play with!

"Be careful!" said the spider crossly.
"You will break my web."

Bonnie scampered off.

She saw a silver trail and
followed it down the path.
At the end of the trail Bonnie
found a snail.

"I want to play!" Bonnie said to
the snail. But the snail hid inside
his shell and wouldn't come out.

Bonnie heard a buzzing noise coming from the flowers. "Will you play with me?" she asked the bee.

"Bees are too busy to play," buzzed the bee.

Three fluffy
ducklings ran up.

"We like to play," they quacked.

But then their mother called to them, and the ducklings tumbled back into the pond to join her.

Bonnie looked into the pond and
saw lots of beautiful golden fish.
She tried to touch one
but it swam away.

"Race you across the lily pads!" croaked the frog. At last Bonnie had someone to play with. She reached out one paw and then the other. The lily pad began to move, and then it began to sink....

Splash!

The fish, the frog, and the ducklings scattered as Bonnie fell into the pond.

For a moment Bonnie was
surrounded by bubbles.
Then a large paw scooped
her up and out of
the cold water.

Bonnie's mother
carried her
wet kitten back
into the
warm kitchen
and licked
her dry.

"You are too little to play outside on your own," Bonnie's mother said.

Safe in the kitchen, Bonnie
told her sisters and
brother about
her adventure.

"Let's play adventures!"
her brother said.

And the kittens played together for the rest of the day–pretending to be frogs and snails and ducklings and fish and busy, buzzy bees.

"It really is time for bed," their mother said at last.
"But I want to play!" said Bonnie.